CLASSIC MOMENTS FROM

Pride and Prejudice

JANE AUSTEN

Published by Ice House Books

Copyright © 2019 Ice House Books
Illustrations by Jocelyn Kao
Original text by Jane Austen

Ice House Books is an imprint of Half Moon Bay Limited
The Ice House, 124 Walcot Street, Bath, BA1 5BG
www.icehousebooks.co.uk

This is a celebration of the novel and not intended as a direct
replica of the original text. Excerpts have been selected and some
text has been omitted to create a collection of well-loved scenes.

ISBN 978-1-912867-31-8

Printed in China

CLASSIC MOMENTS FROM

Pride and Prejudice

JANE AUSTEN

ICE HOUSE BOOKS

From Chapter I

It is a truth universally acknowledged, that a single man in possession of a good fortune ...

... must be in want of a wife.

However little known the feeling or views of such a man may be on his first entering a neighbourhood, this truth is so well fixed in the minds of the surrounding families, that he is considered as the rightful property of some one or other of their daughters.

"My dear Mr. Bennet," said his lady to him one day, "have you heard that Netherfield Park is let at last?"

Mr. Bennet replied that he had not.

"But it is," returned she; "for Mrs. Long has just been here and she told me all about it."

Mr. Bennet made no answer.

"Do not you want to know who has taken it?" cried his wife impatiently.

"You want to tell me and I have no objection to hearing it."

This was invitation enough.

"Why, my dear, you must know, Mrs. Long says that Netherfield is taken by a young man of large fortune from the north of England."

"What is his name?"

"Bingley."

"Is he married or single?"

"Oh! single, my dear, to be sure! A single man of large fortune; four or five thousand a-year. What a fine thing for our girls!"

"How so? how can it affect them?"

"My dear Mr. Bennet," replied his wife, "how can you be so tiresome! you must know that I am thinking of his marrying one of them."

From Chapter III

Mr. Bingley was good-looking and gentlemanlike; he had a pleasant countenance, and easy, unaffected manners. His sisters were fine women, with an air of decided fashion. His brother-in-law, Mr. Hurst, merely looked the gentleman ...

...but his friend Mr. Darcy soon drew the attention of the room...

... by his fine, tall person, handsome features, noble mien, and the report which was in general circulation within five minutes after his entrance, of his having ten thousand a-year. The gentlemen pronounced him to be a fine figure of a man, the ladies declared he was much handsomer than Mr. Bingley, and he was looked at with great admiration for about half the evening, till his manners gave a disgust which turned the tide of his popularity; for he was discovered to be proud, to be above his company, and above being pleased.

[...]

Elizabeth Bennet had obliged, by the scarcity of gentlemen, to sit down for two dances; and during part of that time, Mr. Darcy had been standing near enough for her to overhear a conversation between him and Mr. Bingley, who came from the dance for a few minutes, to press his friend to join it.

"Come, Darcy," said he, "I must have you dance. I hate to see you standing about by yourself in this stupid manner. You had much better dance."

"I certainly shall not. You know how I detest it, unless I am particularly acquainted with my partner. At such an assembly as this it would be insupportable. Your sisters are engaged, and there is not another woman in the room whom it would not be a punishment to me to stand up with."

"I would not be so fastidious as you are," cried Bingley, "for a kingdom! Upon my honour, I never met with so many pleasant girls in my life as I have this evening; and there are several of them you see uncommonly pretty."

"You are dancing with the only handsome girl in the room," said Mr. Darcy, looking at the eldest Miss Bennet.

"Oh! she is the most beautiful creature I ever beheld! But there is one of her sisters sitting down just behind you, who is very pretty, and I dare say very agreeable. Do let me ask my partner to introduce you."

"Which do you mean?" and turning round he looked for a moment at Elizabeth, till catching her eye, he withdrew his own and coldly said …

"She is tolerable, but not handsome enough to tempt me."

"Happiness in marriage is entirely a matter of chance."

"If the dispositions of the parties are ever so well known to each other or ever so similar beforehand, it does not advance their felicity in the least. They always continue to grow sufficiently unlike afterwards to have their share of vexation; and it is better to know as little as possible of the defects of the person with whom you are to pass your life."

"You make me laugh, Charlotte; but it is not sound. You know it is not sound, and that you would never act in this way yourself."

Occupied in observing Mr. Bingley's attentions to her sister, Elizabeth was far from suspecting that she was herself becoming an object of some interest in the eyes of his friend. Mr. Darcy had at first scarcely allowed her to be pretty. But no sooner had he made it clear to himself and his friends that she had hardly a good feature in her face, than he began to find it was rendered uncommonly intelligent by the beautiful expression of her dark eyes. To this discovery succeeded some others equally mortifying.

Though he had detected with a critical eye more than one failure of perfect symmetry in her form, he was forced to acknowledge her figure to be light and pleasing; and in spite of his asserting that her manners were not those of the fashionable world, he was caught by their easy playfulness.

From Chapter XV

Mr. Wickham's appearance was greatly in his favour; he had all the best part of beauty, a fine countenance, a good figure, and very pleasing address. The introduction was followed up on his side by a happy readiness of conversation [...] the whole party were still standing and talking together very agreeably, when the sound of horses drew their notice, and Darcy and Bingley were seen riding down the street. Mr. Darcy was beginning to determine not to fix his eye on Elizabeth, when they were suddenly arrested by the sight of the stranger, and Elizabeth happening to see the countenance of both as they looked at each other, was all astonishment at the effect of the meeting. Both changed colour, one looked white, the other red. Mr. Wickham, after a few moments, touched his hat—a salutation which Mr. Darcy just deigned to return. What could be the meaning of it?— It was impossible to imagine;

... it was impossible not to long to know.

From Chapter XIX

Mr. Collins was not a sensible man. [...]

"Almost as soon as I entered the house, I singled you out as the companion of my future life. And now nothing remains for me but to assure you in the most animated language of the violence of my affection. To fortune I am perfectly indifferent, and shall make no demand of that nature on your father, since I am well aware that it could not be complied with; and that one thousand pounds in the 4 per cents, which will not be yours till after your mother's decease, is all that you may ever be entitled to. On that head, therefore, I shall be uniformly silent."

It was absolutely necessary to interrupt him now.

"You are too hasty, sir," she cried. "You forget that I have made no answer. Let me do it without further loss of time. Accept my thanks for the compliment you are paying me. I am very sensible of the honour of your proposals, but ...

it is impossible for me to do otherwise than decline them."

From Chapter XX

"Oh! Mr. Bennet, you are wanted immediately; we are all in an uproar. You must come and make Lizzy marry Mr. Collins, for she vows she will not have him, and if you do not make haste he will change his mind and not have her."

Mr. Bennet raised his eyes from his book as Mrs. Bennet entered, and fixed them on her face with a calm unconcern which was not in the least altered by her communication.

"I have not the pleasure of understanding you," said he, when she had finished her speech. "Of what are you talking?"

"Of Mr. Collins and Lizzy. Lizzy declares she will not have Mr. Collins, and Mr. Collins begins to say that he will not have Lizzy."

"And what am I to do on the occasion?—It seems a hopeless business."

"Speak to Lizzy about it yourself. Tell her that you insist upon her marrying him."

"Let her be called down. She shall hear my opinion."

Mrs. Bennet rang the bell, and Miss Elizabeth was summoned to the library.

[...]

"Very well. We now come to the point. Your mother insists upon your accepting. Is it not so, Mrs. Bennet?"

"Yes, or I will never see her again."

"An unhappy alternative is before you, Elizabeth. From this day you must be a stranger to one of your parents. Your mother will never see you again if you do not marry Mr. Collins ...

... and I will never see you again if you do."

From Chapter XXXIII

"Mr. Darcy is uncommonly kind to Mr. Bingley, and takes a prodigious deal of care of him," said Elizabeth.

"Care of him!—Yes, I really believe Darcy does take care of him in those points where he most wants care. From something that he told me in our journey hither, I have reason to think Bingley very much indebted to him," said Colonel Fitzwilliam.

"What is it you mean?"

"It is a circumstance which Darcy of course could not wish to be generally known, because if it were to get round to the lady's family, it would be an unpleasant thing."

"You may depend upon my not mentioning it."

"What he told me was merely this: that he congratulated himself on having lately ...

... saved a friend from the inconveniences of a most imprudent marriage ...

... but without mentioning names or any other particulars, and I only suspected it to be Bingley from believing him the kind of young man to get into a scrape of that sort, and from knowing them to have been together the whole of last summer."

"Did Mr. Darcy give you his reasons for this interference?"

"I understand that there were some very strong objections against the lady."

"And what arts did he use to separate them?"

"He did not talk to me of his own arts," said Fitzwilliam, smiling.

From Chapter XXXIV

Mr. Darcy sat down for a few moments, and then getting up, walked about the room. Elizabeth was surprised, but said not a word.

"In vain have I struggled. It will not do. My feelings will not be repressed. You must allow me to tell you …

… how ardently I admire and love you."

Elizabeth's astonishment was beyond expression. She stared, coloured, doubted, and was silent. This he considered sufficient encouragement; and the avowal of all that he felt, and had long felt for her, immediately followed.

In spite of her deeply-rooted dislike, she could not be insensible to the compliment of such a man's affection, and though her intentions did not vary for an instant, she was at first sorry for the pain he was to receive.

He spoke of apprehension and anxiety, but his countenance expressed real security. Such a circumstance could only exasperate farther, and, when he ceased, the colour rose in her cheeks, and she said—

"In such cases as this, it is, I believe, the established mode to express a sense of obligation for the sentiments avowed, however unequally they may be returned. It is natural that obligation should be felt, and if I could feel gratitude, I would now thank you. But I cannot—I have never desired your good opinion, and you have certainly bestowed it most unwillingly. I am sorry to have occasioned pain to anyone. It has been most unconsciously done, however, and I hope will be of short duration."

[...]

"From the very beginning—from the first moment, I may almost say—of my acquaintance with you, your manners, impressing me with the fullest belief of your arrogance, your conceit, and your selfish disdain of the feelings of others, were such as to form the ground work of disapprobation on which succeeding events have built so immovable a dislike; and I had not known you a month before I felt that ...

... you were the last man in the world whom I could ever be prevailed on to marry."

"You have said quite enough, madam. I perfectly comprehend your feelings, and have now only to be ashamed of what my own have been. Forgive me for having taken up so much of your time, and accept my best wishes for your health and happiness."

And with these words he hastily left the room, and Elizabeth heard him the next moment open the front door and quit the house.

The tumult of her mind was now painfully great. She knew not how to support herself, and from actual weakness sat down and cried for half-an-hour. Her astonishment, as she reflected on what had passed, was increased by every review of it. That she should receive an offer of marriage from Mr. Darcy! that he should have been in love with her for so many months!—so much in love as to wish to marry her.

From Chapter XLIII

Elizabeth, as they drove along, watched for the first appearance of Pemberley Woods with some perturbation; and when at length they turned in at the lodge, her spirits were in a high flutter.

They gradually ascended for half-a-mile, and then found themselves at the top of a considerable eminence, where the wood ceased, and the eye was instantly caught by Pemberley House, situated on the opposite side of the valley, into which the road with some abruptness wound. It was a large, handsome stone building, standing well on rising ground, and backed by a ridge of high woody hills; and in front, a stream of some natural importance was swelled into greater, but without any artificial appearance. They were all of them warm in their admiration; and at that moment ...

... she felt that to be mistress of Pemberley might be something!

From Chapter LI

"Lizzy, I never gave you an account of my wedding, I believe," said Lydia. "Just as the carriage came to the door, my uncle was called away upon business to that horrid man, Mr. Stone. And then, you know, when once they get together, there is no end of it. Well, I was so frightened, I did not know what to do; for my uncle was to give me away; and if we were beyond the hour Wickham and I could not be married all day. But, luckily, he came back again in ten minutes' time, and then we all set out. However, I recollected afterwards, that if he had been prevented going, the wedding need not be put off …

… for Mr. Darcy might have done as well."

"Mr. Darcy!" repeated Elizabeth, in utter amazement. "Oh, yes!—he was to come there with Wickham, you know. But, gracious me! I quite forgot! I ought not to have said a word about it. I promised them so faithfully!"

But to live in ignorance on such a point was impossible; or, at least, it was impossible not to try for information. Mr. Darcy had been at her sister's wedding. It was exactly a scene, and exactly among people, where he had apparently least to do, and least temptation to go. Conjectures as to the meaning of it, rapid and wild, hurried into her brain; but she was satisfied with none. Those that best pleased her, as placing his conduct in the noblest, seemed most improbable. She could not bear such suspense; and hastily seizing a sheet of paper, wrote a short letter to her aunt, to request an explanation of what Lydia had dropped, if it were compatible with the secrecy which had been intended.

From Chapter LII

"Darcy saw Wickham, and afterwards insisted on seeing Lydia. His first object with her, he acknowledged, had been to persuade her to quit her present disgraceful situation, and return to her friends as soon as they could be prevailed on to receive her, offering his assistance as far as it would go. But he found Lydia absolutely resolved on remaining where she was. Since such were her feelings, it only remained, he thought, to secure and expedite a marriage, which, in his very first conversation with Wickham, he easily learnt had been his design.

"They met several times, for there was much to be discussed. Wickham, of course, wanted more than he could get, but at length was reduced to be reasonable.

"You know pretty well, I suppose, what has been done for the young people. His debts are to be paid, amounting, I believe, to considerably more than a thousand pounds, another thousand in addition to her own settled upon *her*, and his commission purchased."

The contents of her aunt's letter threw Elizabeth into a flutter of sprits, in which it was difficult to determine whether pleasure or pain bore the greatest share. The vague and unsettled suspicions which uncertainty had produced of what Mr. Darcy might have been doing to forward her sister's match, which she had feared to encourage as an exertion of goodness too great to be probable, and at the same time dreaded to be just, from the pain of obligation, were proved beyond their greatest extent to be true! He had done all this for a girl whom he could neither regard nor esteem.

Her heart did whisper that he had done it for her.

From Chapter LIV

Her mother's ungraciousness made the sense of what they owed Darcy more painful to Elizabeth's mind; and she would, at times, have given anything to be privileged to tell him that his kindness was neither unknown nor unfelt by the whole of the family.

She was in hopes that the evening would afford some opportunity of bringing them together; that the whole of the visit would not pass away without enabling them to enter into something more of conversation, than the mere ceremonious salutations attending his entrance. Anxious and uneasy, the period which passed in the drawing-room, before the gentlemen came, was wearisome and dull to a degree that almost made her uncivil. She looked forward to their entrance as the point on which all her chance of pleasure for the evening must depend.

"If he does not come to me then," said she, "I shall give him up forever."

[...]

Darcy had walked away to another part of the room. She followed him with her eyes, envied everyone to whom he spoke, had scarcely patience enough to help anybody to coffee, and then was enraged against herself for being so silly!

"A man who has once been refused. How could I ever ...

... be foolish enough to expect a renewal of his love?

Is there one among the sex who would not protest against such a weakness as a second proposal to the same woman? There is no indignity so abhorrent to their feelings!"

From Chapter LVIII

"You are too generous to trifle with me. If your feelings are still what they were last April, tell me so at once.

My affections and wishes are unchanged ...

... but one word from you will silence me on this subject forever."

Elizabeth, feeling all the more than common awkwardness and anxiety of his situation, now forced herself to speak; and immediately, though not very fluently, gave him to understand that her sentiments had undergone so material a change since the period to which he alluded, as to make her receive with gratitude and pleasure his present assurances. The happiness which this reply produced was such as he had probably never felt before, and he expressed himself on the occasion as sensibly and as warmly as a man violently in love can be supposed to do.

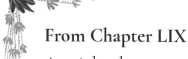

From Chapter LIX

At night she opened her heart to Jane.

"You are joking, Lizzy. This cannot be!—engaged to Mr. Darcy!—No, no, you shall not deceive me. I know it to be impossible."

"This is a wretched beginning indeed! My sole dependence was on you; and I am sure nobody else will believe me, if you do not. Yet, indeed, I am in earnest. I speak nothing but the truth. He still loves me, and we are engaged."

Jane looked at her doubtingly. "Oh, Lizzy! it cannot be. I know how much you dislike him."

"You know nothing of the matter. That is all to be forgot. Perhaps I did not always love him so well as I do now. But in such cases as these a good memory is unpardonable. This is the last time I shall ever remember it myself."

Miss Bennet still looked all amazement. Elizabeth again, and more seriously, assured her of its truth.

"It is settled between us already that we are to be the happiest couple in the world. But are you pleased, Jane? Shall you like to have such a brother?"

"Very, very much. Nothing could give either Bingley or myself more delight. Oh, Lizzy! do anything rather than marry without affection. Are you quite sure that you feel what you ought to do?"

"Oh, yes! You will only think I feel more than I ought to do, when I tell you."

"What do you mean?"

"Why I must confess that I love him better than I do Bingley. I am afraid you will be angry."

"My dearest sister, now be, be serious. I want to talk very seriously. Let me know everything that I am to know, without delay. Will you tell me how long you have loved him?"

"It has been coming on so gradually, that I hardly know when it began."

[...]

Her father was walking about the room, looking grave and anxious. "Lizzy," said he, what are you doing? are you out of your senses, to be accepting this man? Have not you always hated him?"

How earnestly did she then wish that her former opinions had been more reasonable, her expressions more moderate!

"Or, in other words, you are determined to have him. He is rich, to be sure, and you may have more fine clothes and fine carriages than Jane. But will they make you happy?"

"Have you any other objection," said Elizabeth, "than your belief of my indifference?"

"None at all. We all know him to be a proud, unpleasant sort of man; but this would be nothing if you really liked him."

"I do, I do like him," she replied, with tears in her eyes; "I love him. Indeed he has no improper pride. He is perfectly amiable. You do not know what he really is;

then pray do not pain me by speaking of him in such terms."

"Lizzy," said her father, "I have given him my consent. He is the kind of man, indeed, to whom I should never dare refuse anything which he condescended to ask."

Elizabeth, still more affected, was earnest and solemn in her reply.

"Well, my dear," said he, when she ceased speaking, "I have no more to say. If this be the case, he deserves you ...

... I could not have parted with you my Lizzy, to anyone less worthy."

[...]

"If any young men come for Mary or Kitty, send them in, for I am quite at my leisure."

From Chapter LXI

Happy for all her maternal feelings was the day on which Mrs. Bennet got rid of her two most deserving daughters. With what delighted pride she afterwards visited Mrs. Bingley, and talked of Mrs. Darcy, may be guessed. I wish I could say, for the sake of her family, that the accomplishment of her earnest desire in the establishment of so many of her children produced so happy an effect as to make her a sensible, amiable, well-informed woman for the rest of her life; though, perhaps, it was lucky for her husband, who might not have relished domestic felicity in so unusual a form, that she still was occasionally nervous, and invariably silly.

Mr. Bennet missed his second daughter exceedingly; his affection for her drew him oftener from home than anything else could do. He delighted in going to Pemberley ...

... *especially when he was least expected.*

[...]

Lady Catherine was extremely indignant on the marriage of her nephew, Darcy; and as she gave way to all the genuine frankness of her character, in her reply to the letter which announced its arrangement, she sent him language so very abusive, especially of Elizabeth, that for some time all intercourse was at an end. But at length, by Elizabeth's persuasion, he was prevailed on to overlook the offense, and seek a reconciliation.

With the Gardiners they were always on the most intimate terms. Darcy, as well as Elizabeth, really loved them; and they were both ever sensible of the warmest gratitude towards the persons who, by bringing her into Derbyshire ...

... had been the means of uniting them.